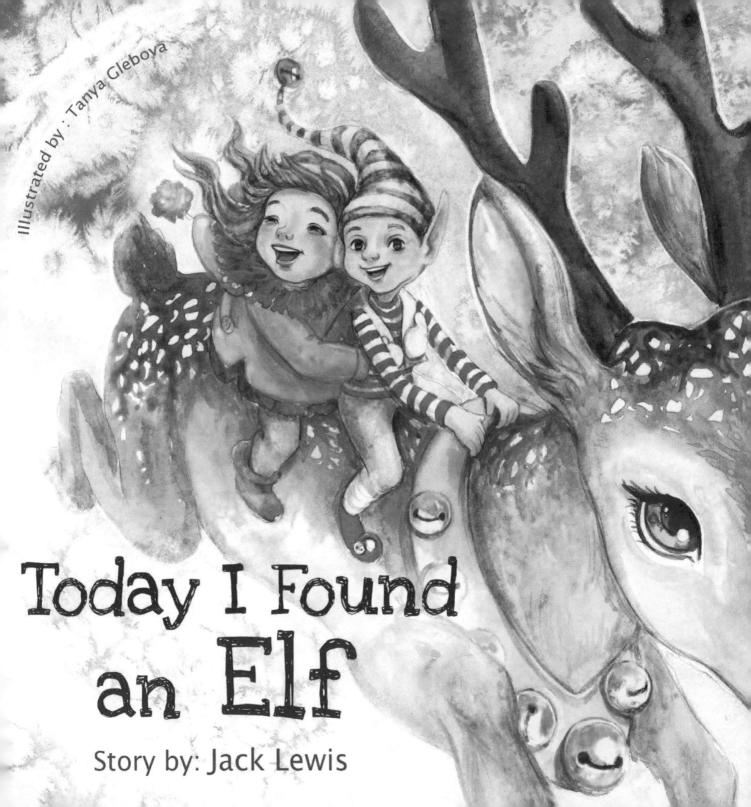

Illustrated by : Tanya Gleboya

Today I Found an Elf

Story by: Jack Lewis

For information contact:
Starry Dreamer Publishing, LLC
1603 Capitol Ave. Suite 310 A377
Cheyenne, Wyoming 82001
starrydreamerpub@gmail.com

Written by Jack Lewis
Illustrations by Tanya Glebova

ISBN: 978-1-952328-64-0 (Paperback) 978-1-952328-59-6 (Hardback)
        978-1-952328-61-9 (Digital)
Library of Congress Cataloging-in-Publication Data is available
10 9 8 7 6 5 4 3 2 1
First Edition: November 2021

STARRY DREAMER PUBLISHING

Today I found an Elf; he was sitting
under a tree in our backyard.

"Hello there," I said.
"Are you a Christmas Elf?"

"I am, but not a very good one," he replied.
He hugged a large sack near him and began to cry.

"Whatever is the matter, Mr. Elf?" I asked.
"It's Christmas Eve and a time to be happy."

"My name is Jangles, and I'm afraid that I forgot to pack these gifts for Santa on his sleigh."

He opened the bag. "He's already left the North Pole and I've been looking everywhere, but I can't find him. I need to get these presents to him before the night is over."

"Oh, I see," I said. "Christmas isn't really about presents and toys."

"I know, but this was my first year to pack the sleigh and I wanted to do a good job," he said.

"Would you like me to help you look for him," I asked?

Jangles wiped his eyes and smiled. "Would you, really?"

"Sure! We might find him faster if we both look for him. Then, you can give him those gifts to deliver. It has always been my wish to meet Santa!"

"Thank you very much!" said Jangles. "We can ride on my reindeer and search for him together."

I was so surprised! "I get to ride on a real reindeer?"

"Of course," Jangles laughed. "Meet Holly, she's a flying reindeer."

We hopped onto Holly's back. She snorted, pawed the ground, then took off into the sky. We soared over the tops of the pine trees. I could see all the little houses with their twinkling Christmas lights far below us.

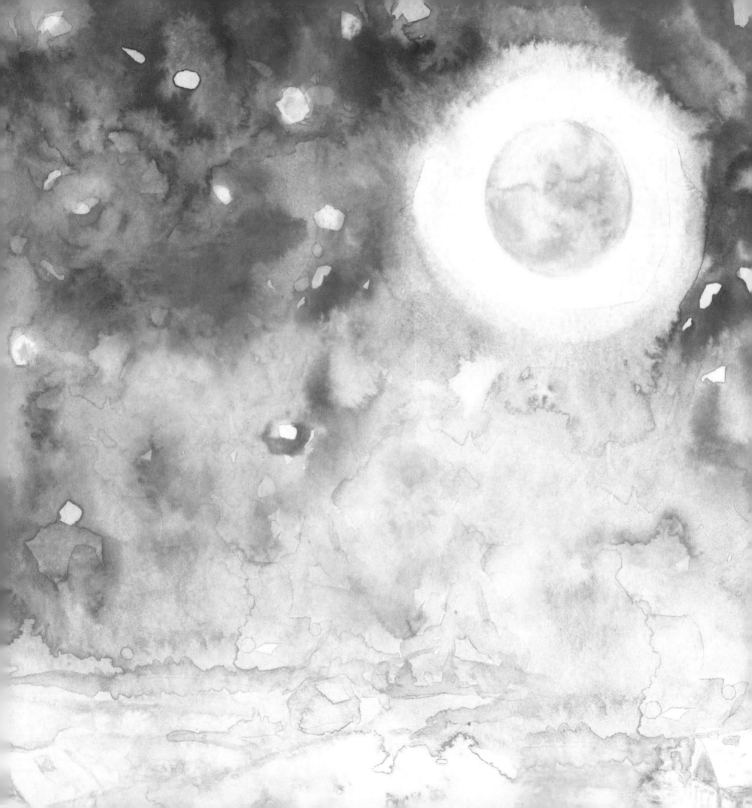

"I think Santa should be around here about now,"
Jangles said as we flew over a little town by a forest.

"I see his sleigh!" I excitedly called out.
"On the roof of that blue house there!"

Jangles laughed with joy. "Yes, that's him!"

Holly circled down to the roof where Santa's sleigh was waiting. The other reindeer happily snorted when they saw Holly.

I couldn't believe it was Santa's famous reindeers! And Rudolph too!

At that very moment, out of the chimney popped Santa himself. He was wearing his bright red suit and had a big sack of presents slung over his shoulder. My Christmas wish to meet Santa was coming true!

"Ho, ho, ho, there Jangles!" Santa waved, then looked at me and smiled. "And hello to you too!" Santa stroked his white beard. "Now, what are the two of you doing here?"

"I'm sorry Santa," Jangles looked at his feet, then patted the sack. "I forgot to pack these gifts on your sleigh."

Santa shook his belly with a jolly laugh. "Ho, ho, ho! Well, you're here now and I'm proud of you for getting these back to me."

He hugged me and winked. "Now that I've answered your Christmas wish, I must get back to work. Ho, ho, ho!"

"Jangles, can I depend on you and Holly to get her safely back home?" Santa asked.

"Yes, you can, Santa!" Jangles smiled and turned to me. "Let's go!"

I climbed onto Holly's back and waved goodbye. "Thank you for letting me meet you, Santa!"

As Holly leaped into the air, I watched Santa wave to us.
Over the sound of the wind, I heard him shout,
"Merry Christmas to all, and to all a good night!"

Today I found a Christmas Elf and had a wonderful adventure. I wonder what I will find tomorrow…

Enjoy these other great books by JACK LEWIS:

Never Bring a Zebracorn to School

Joy to the World: The Best Christmas Gift Ever

Wonderful World of Animals Series

Take a trip around the world to find the wildest, weirdest, and most adorable animals on the planet!

The Cutest Animals of the World

The Weirdest Animals of the World

Dangerous Animals of the World

Funny Animals of the World

Today I Found... Series

Magical children's stories of friendship and the power of imagination!

Today I Found a Unicorn

Today I Found a Mermaid

Today I Found an Elf

Fun with Family Series

A wonderful way to celebrate each special person in our families!

I Love My Mommy

Printed in the USA
CPSIA information can be obtained
at www.ICGtesting.com
LVHW070221031123
762970LV00013B/25